PINGU

and the Birthday Present

Ritts

verite
pitts

BBC CHILDREN'S BOOKS

It was Grandpa's birthday, and Pingu
didn't know what to buy for him.
He wanted to get him a very special
present, but he couldn't decide
what Grandpa would like most.

"Buy some fresh bread,"
said the baker. Pingu looked
at the bread, shook his head
and walked on.

Soon he came to the fish stall. As he was walking past, the fishmonger said, "Buy some fish, fresh from the sea."

Pingu didn't look very impressed. "Hmm," he said.

The fishmonger showed him a very strange looking fish. "These are on special offer today," he said.

"Yuk! No thank you," said Pingu and he hurried on.

"Oh dear," thought Pingu to himself sadly. "I'm never going to find anything for Grandpa's birthday." Just then, he came to a shop with beautiful shells in the window. "They're the most fantastic shells I've ever seen," he said as he gazed at them. "That's what I want to buy for Grandpa."

Inside the shop there were rows and rows of the wonderful shells. Pingu stared all around. He couldn't take his eyes off them.

Eventually, he decided
which one he wanted to
buy for Grandpa.

"I think I'd like that
one," he said, pointing
to an unusual spiky
shell.

The shopkeeper tied up the shell in a pretty box.
"That will cost you one fish, please."
"Here you are," said Pingu. "Thank you."

"Thank you," said the shopkeeper and she picked up the fish and started to eat it. Pingu picked up the pretty box and set off for Grandpa's house.

As Pingu came out of the shop, he saw Pinga on her way to see Grandpa. Her parcel looked much bigger than his.

"Hey, Pinga," he shouted. "What have you got there?"

"It's Grandpa's birthday present," said Pinga. "I'm going to give it to him now. Do you want to come with me?"

"No thanks," said Pingu. "There's something I have to do first."

As soon as Pinga had gone,
Pingu ran back into the shop.
"I need a bigger box, please,"
he said to the shopkeeper.
She looked under the counter
and brought out a bright
green box.

"Will this do?" she asked.

Pingu thought for a moment
and then shook his head.
"No," he said. "It needs
to be much bigger than
that. About this big," he
said, stretching his wings
out wide.

"How about this one, then?" she asked.

"It's very nice, but it's just not big enough. It needs to be *really* big," said Pingu. "Haven't you got one?" he asked, worriedly.

The shopkeeper thought for a moment. "I have two big boxes outside. I could let you have those."

Pingu's face lit up. "That's perfect!" he cried.

Meanwhile, Pinga had arrived at Grandpa's house. "Hello, Grandpa," she called. "Happy birthday!" Then she gave him his present.

"Is that for me?" asked Grandpa. "How kind!"

Pinga watched excitedly
as Grandpa unwrapped her
present. "It's lovely," he said
as he hung it on the wall.
   "It's a picture of you,"
she said.

15

Then Pinga sang "Happy Birthday" to Grandpa.
He was delighted.

Just then, the doorbell rang and Pingu walked in. He was carrying an enormous box tied up with gold ribbon.

"Happy birthday, Grandpa!" he said.

"What's in that box?" asked Pinga.

"You'll have to wait and see," replied Pingu. "Open it, Grandpa!"

Grandpa picked up the
enormous box and put it on
the table. "Hmm," he said.
"Whatever can this be?"
He untied the ribbon and
lifted off the lid. Inside
was another box!

18

"Hmm," said Grandpa. "Very interesting." He opened the second box to see what was inside. "Another box," he said. Pingu laughed happily to himself.

Grandpa began to wonder if he would ever find his birthday present. He opened the bright green box and nestling inside it was a pretty oval box with a ribbon around it. Grandpa opened the oval box, and there inside lay the beautiful shell.

"Ooh!" said Pinga. "It's so pretty!"

"What a lovely present," said
Grandpa. "Thank you, Pingu.
It is very beautiful."

"I'm glad that you like it,"
said Pingu.

21

Grandpa looked around at his room. It was completely covered in wrapping paper, ribbons and boxes. He didn't have room to move!

"Oh dear," he said to Pingu and Pinga. "I think it's time we did some tidying up."

Pingu had started to feel guilty for using all those boxes he didn't really need. "I'm sorry, Grandpa," he said. "I just didn't think."

"That's all right," said Grandpa. "We can bundle everything up together and take it back to the shop. Then it can be used by somebody else."

The three penguins began
to tidy up. Pinga collected all
the ribbons and put them
neatly into one box. Pingu
rolled up all the wrapping
paper, and Grandpa put the
lids back on all the boxes.

25

Pingu wanted to carry all the boxes on his own. He piled them up on top of each other and lifted the huge load up, but he couldn't carry them properly.

"I think you should let Pinga carry something," said Grandpa.

Pingu took the smallest box off the top of the pile and gave it to his sister. "Here you are," he said. "You can carry this one."

When they got to the
shell shop, Grandpa
opened the door and
called the shopkeeper.

"Hello!" he cried.
The shopkeeper came
to the door.

"We've brought some boxes back for you so that you can use them again," said Grandpa. Pingu and Pinga put their boxes down.

"Thank you very much," she said. "They'll be very useful."

29

Pingu was delighted that she could use the boxes again.

"Come on, then," he cried. "Let's go back to Grandpa's!"

Once they got back to the house, Grandpa sat down with Pingu and Pinga and he looked at his lovely presents.

"What a lucky penguin I am," he said.

"And we're lucky that you're our Grandpa," said Pingu. "Happy birthday!"

other PINGU books available from BBC Children's Books:

Pingu and his Family
Pingu and his Friends
Pingu and the Seal
Pingu Has a Hard Time
Pingu Has Fun
Pingu in Trouble
Pingu the Adventurer
Pingu the Chef
Pingu the Sportsman
Pingu the Star

Pingu the Postman Wheelie Book
Pingu Lift-the-Flap Book

Fun with Pingu Activity Book
Fun with Pingu Colouring Book

Pingu Chunky Books
Pingu and his Family
Pingu and his Grandpa
Pingu and the Seal
Pingu and his Sister

Published by BBC Children's Books
a division of BBC Enterprises Limited
Woodlands, 80 Wood Lane, London W12 0TT
First published 1994
Text © 1994 BBC Children's Books
Stills © 1994 Editoy/SRG/BBC Enterprises
Design © 1994 BBC Children's Books
Pingu © 1994 Editoy/SRG/BBC Enterprises

ISBN 0 563 40349 7

Typeset by BBC Children's Books
Colour separations by DOT Gradations, Chelmsford
Printed and bound by Cambus Litho, East Kilbride